Tada, Joni Eareckson
Forever friends

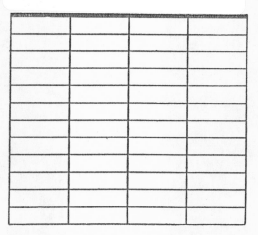

DEMCO

FOREVER FRIENDS

PRESENTED TO

_____

FROM

_____

DATE

_____

FOREVER FRIENDS

Joni Eareckson Tada & Melody Carlson

ILLUSTRATIONS BY DOUGLAS KLAUBA

CROSSWAY BOOKS · WHEATON, ILLINOIS · A DIVISION OF GOOD NEWS PUBLISHERS

Forever Friends

Text copyright © 2000 by Joni Eareckson Tada and Melody Carlson

Illustrations copyright © 2000 by Douglas Klauba

Published by Crossway Books

a division of Good News Publishers

1300 Crescent Street

Wheaton, Illinois 60187

Book design: Cindy Kiple

Illustrations: Douglas Klauba

First printing 2000

Printed in the United States of America

ISBN 1-58134-216-0

FOR ABBEY MUZIO
MY FOREVER FRIEND

Joni

TO MY BEST
"EARTHLY" FOREVER FRIEND,
CHRISTOPHER DOUGLAS CARLSON

Melody

If you go all the way down Periwinkle Lane (just past the White Goose Bakery), you will come to Mr. Giovanni's Toy Shoppe. Now Mr. Giovanni's shop is no ordinary toy store. No-sir-ee! You won't find a single video game or computerized gadget—not even a remote-control race car. That's because Mr. Giovanni is an old-fashioned sort of guy who runs an old-fashioned sort of toy shop.

But come on along and see what's inside. Some very special things happen right here in Mr. Giovanni's toy shop—some wonderful things that most people don't know about!

"Perfect!" exclaimed Mr. Giovanni, as he held up a pretty porcelain doll. Her taffy-colored hair hung in loose curls around her shoulders, and her shiny eyes sparkled brightly against her smooth face. "Your eyes are as clear as the ocean on a sunny day," he said. "And your smile reminds me of my own dear girl when she was just a little tot. Therefore, I think I shall name you Jenny after her." He straightened her gingham dress and adjusted the laces on her tiny leather shoes. With care he placed this new doll on the front shelf with all the other porcelain dolls.

"The prettiest of the bunch," he said with a wink. Then he returned to his workbench to repair a broken toy train engine.

Jenny sat stiffly on the wooden shelf. Careful not to even blink, she stared at the shop before her with curiosity. You see, dolls and other toys are not allowed to move when people are watching, so during the day they all remain quiet and hold completely still.

So many, many toys! Jenny thought with joy. *Surely I will make lots and lots of friends here!* And more than anything in the whole world, Jenny wanted a friend!

Now, as all toys know, when the people leave and the lights go down, the toy world springs to life. At last the moment Jenny had been waiting for arrived! Mr. Giovanni had barely turned the key in the lock before Jenny stood up and stretched her stiff arms and legs.

"Goodness," she said. "I thought he would never leave." She turned to the dark-haired doll right next to her and smiled. The pretty doll smoothed the red satin folds of her full skirt and yawned daintily.

"What a lovely dress!" exclaimed Jenny brightly. "My name is Jenny, and I'm new here."

The other doll frowned. "Jenny? Would that be short for Jennifer?"

"I don't know. But Mr. Giovanni named me after his very own daughter. Wasn't that nice of him?"

The other doll rolled her dark, glassy eyes. "Well, I suppose a simple name like Jenny goes well with your plain dress. But *my* name is Felicia, and *that* is a proper name for a proper young lady."

Jenny peered curiously at Felicia and then spoke in her most polite voice. "Would you like to be my friend and play with me, Felicia?"

"*Hardly!*" Felicia folded her arms across her front and spoke in a proud voice. "Playing might spoil my beautiful dress."

Jenny looked down at her own plain dress and then turned to the pretty blonde doll sitting on her other side. The blonde doll's velveteen dress was the color of a robin's egg. "How about you?" asked Jenny with her brightest smile. "Do *you* want to play with me?"

This doll blinked her blue eyes in surprise. "*Play?* Why we never play."

"You *never* play?" asked Jenny in surprise. "But why not?"

The blonde doll turned up her nose. "Playing would muss up our hair or tear our lovely gowns. Then what little girl would want to buy us and take us home with her?"

Jenny frowned. "Then what do you do all night?"

"We just sit and talk."

"Talk?" asked Jenny. "About what?"

"About all the other silly toys, of course," said Felicia with a flip of a curl.

"Yes," agreed the blonde doll, pointing to a toy down below. "For instance, look at that frumpy-looking rabbit over there. Why, he isn't even new!"

Well, Jenny didn't want to sit around and do nothing but talk about other toys. Besides being mean, it sounded pretty boring to her. So she climbed down from her shelf and decided to search the shop for someone to play with.

"May I play with you?" she asked the toy soldiers.

"Do you know how to march and salute?" demanded the leader.

Jenny blinked. "No, but I could try—"

"Forget it!" he shouted. "We don't need silly girls in our army!"

Jenny just shook her head. Next she found a stuffed dog. "May I play with you?" she asked him sweetly.

"No way!" yipped the dog. "You don't have a tail. You don't have fur like me. You don't even know how to chase a ball or fetch a stick."

Jenny just shook her head and walked away.

After several tries at making a new friend, Jenny finally sat down in a small wooden rocking chair. It seemed that none of the toys wanted to play with her.

"Hello there, Jenny," said a soft, friendly voice.

She looked up to see the same stuffed rabbit that the blonde doll had made fun of. And to tell the truth, he *was* rather frumpy, and even sort of goofy-looking with his black button eyes sewn too closely together and one limp ear flopping down over his nose. But not wanting to be rude, Jenny spoke to him. "How do you know my name?"

He pushed the floppy ear away from his face. "I have good ears."

"Oh." She studied him closely, wondering what he wanted.

"My name is Rabbie," he said with a shy smile. "And I noticed that you're new here. I thought maybe you could use a friend."

Well, Jenny really wanted a friend, but she wasn't so sure this Rabbie fellow was the kind of friend she wanted.

"You look sort of worn out and used," Jenny said honestly to the rabbit. "And the doll said that you're not even a new toy."

"That's right," said Rabbie, standing up straighter. "But being new doesn't mean you're better than anyone else. In fact, I've found that being old is pretty terrific."

"And why is that?" asked Jenny, trying not to laugh at his funny, large front teeth.

"For one thing, I know my way around," said Rabbie proudly. "And for another, I know how to just be myself and have a good time. But maybe the best thing is that I know how to treat others right."

She nodded. "Well, that sounds like a good thing."

Rabbie nodded and smiled.

"But if you're not new," asked Jenny, her curiosity getting the better of her, "then why are you in Mr. Giovanni's Toy Shoppe?"

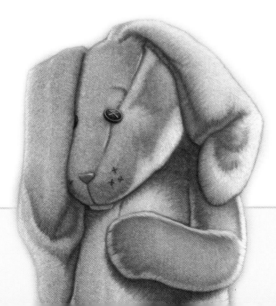

"I used to belong to Mr. Giovanni's little girl," explained Rabbie, his eyes growing soft and dreamy. "She was my *very* best friend, but she's all grown up now. You know, her name was Jenny too."

Jenny smiled brightly. "That's right. Mr. Giovanni named me after her."

"I know," said Rabbie shyly, "and your smile reminds me of her."

"So I've heard." But Jenny's smile faded. She wasn't sure what she thought about this shabby Rabbie fellow. "But I still don't understand *why* you're here in the Toy Shoppe?"

"Well, I was in an old box that Mr. Giovanni's cleaning lady had set out for the trash man," continued Rabbie. "But then Mr. Giovanni rescued me along with a couple of other toys that Jenny had outgrown. He thinks we're very special, and he would never sell us. He keeps us on our own shelf right behind his workbench—"

"You mean the trash shelf," called Felicia from her shelf just above them, and all the other porcelain dolls laughed loudly at her mean joke.

Rabbie's face grew sad, and Jenny instantly felt sorry for him. What right did Felicia and those other dolls have to be so cruel? After all, Rabbie did seem like a pretty nice fellow even if he was a little odd, and it seemed that Mr. Giovanni thought he was special. Besides that, he was the first toy to treat Jenny kindly. And she *did* want a friend.

"I guess I'd like to play with you," she said in a shy voice.

"Really?" asked Rabbie, his button eyes growing bright with hope.

"Yes!" And she hopped up from the chair and grabbed his furry paw. "It's pretty boring just sitting around and doing nothing. Let's go have some fun!"

"Don't play with him, Jenny!" warned Felicia from her shelf. "You'll mess up your hair and ruin your dress!"

"Oh, let her go," said another doll, smoothing a spotless white dress of fine silk. "Who cares if no one wants to buy Jenny and take her home. That just means our chances will be all the better!"

"That's right," agreed the blonde doll. "Go ahead, Jenny. Play your silly games with that frumpy old rabbit. Just don't come crying to us when your dress is torn and stained and your hair is all tangled! And don't start whining when no little girl wants you!"

Jenny looked up at the beautiful dolls with their perfect hair and fancy dresses. Maybe her dress wasn't frilly like theirs, but it was fresh and new and clean. Were they right? Was she ruining her chances of going home with a little girl? She looked at Rabbie, and he just shrugged in a goofy sort of way. "I don't know what to do," she finally said.

"Like I always say," suggested Rabbie tapping his chest, "just follow your heart."

She grinned. "Okay then. My heart wants a friend, and I'd like to play with you."

And that's just what Jenny did. First she and Rabbie rode on the toy train. Then they slid down the little slide. They climbed on the giant blocks, played catch and croquet, and finally they flopped down exhausted onto a miniature couch. With happy smiles and arms flopped around each other's shoulders, they rested for a while.

"That was such fun," said Jenny breathlessly. "Thanks for inviting me to play."

"I'm glad you joined me," said Rabbie. "I think we're going to be good friends."

"So do I," agreed Jenny happily.

Felicia sneered from her place on the doll shelf. "Look at those two! That Jenny is just as ridiculous as that silly rabbit now!"

"And can you believe she calls that ragged old thing her *friend?*" said the blonde doll in disgust.

"Yuck!" said another doll. "Imagine having a frumpy rabbit like *that* for your friend!"

Jenny watched Rabbie's face become sad. Then she leaped to her feet and stared up at the thoughtless dolls. Her smooth porcelain cheeks grew rosy with anger.

"Please!" said Jenny in a big, loud voice that surprised even her. In that same moment, every single toy in the shop stopped playing, and all eyes turned to her as she continued to speak. "Do *not* talk about my friend like that! Rabbie is smart and lots of fun. And best of all, *he* knows how to be a good friend. It's too bad that none of you dolls up there have a friend as kind and as good as Rabbie."

And for a pleasant change, all the dolls on the shelf remained amazingly quiet. Then Jenny turned to her new friend, and taking his paw, she said, "I mean every word of it, Rabbie. You are the only one in this whole shop, besides Mr. Giovanni, who's made me feel welcome and loved. And I promise to be your good friend from now on!"

Rabbie gave her a big, warm hug. "Friends forever!" he said joyfully.

"Forever friends!" agreed Jenny with a happy smile.

MY MESSAGE TO YOU

Hello! My name is Joni, and I'm one of the authors of this book.

Have you ever felt strange and lonely in a new place? Like your first day at kindergarten? Or your first time in a new Sunday school class? All the kids seemed to know each other, but no one knew you. I've felt that way. Many years ago when I was paralyzed in an accident and had to be in a wheelchair, I spent a long time in a hospital. I was scared. I was lonely. I needed a friend!

I looked for friends in the hospital, but everyone was too busy. I almost made friends with a young man who was also in a wheelchair—but he and his friends teased me because I couldn't push my wheelchair as fast as they could push theirs. At night I would go back to my room and cry.

I prayed, "Lord Jesus, would You please give me a friend? I don't want to feel lonely and different." God answered my prayer by introducing me to Steve, a tall, thin boy from my school. He was much younger than I was, and, well . . . at first I thought he was a little goofy (like Rabbie). Steve

Joni with one of her very special friends

showed me many wonderful things in the Bible and that made me feel a lot better. We became fast friends (he wasn't goofy anymore). Then there were Eddie and Diana. They made skis to put on my wheelchair so I could go out in the snow; and they lifted me into a canoe so Eddie could paddle me down a river. My friends wheeled me on the beach so the waves could lap over my chair. Boy, did we have fun!

I didn't feel lonely anymore. I was glad that God had answered my prayer, plus I discovered that I could help my friends in special ways, too! I'd tell them, "Jump on my chair!" and we'd go for rides. I'd tell them fun stories and pray with them. If someone had a problem, I was always glad to listen and help out. And because we did so many wild and wonderful things together, our friendships grew strong and deep.

It's great to be friends with people who are not exactly like you. Are you like Jenny, looking for a friend? Maybe your new friend is someone like Rabbie— a boy in your class who is tall and thin or a little girl who wears really thick glasses. It could be a kid who uses crutches or just someone that everybody else seems to pick on. Can you think of some kids who might tease you if you reached out and made friends with someone like that?

Joni with her friend Abbey Muzio, to whom she dedicated this book

Joni with her forever friend— her husband, Ken

Don't be afraid of boys and girls who don't understand. Remember that Jesus was always shaking hands and making friends with people who were different. Jesus was always looking for people to give His smile to. He was always reaching out with love and acceptance—and He wants us to do the same.

You see, when we show God's love by giving a happy smile to someone who's different or by saying, "Hi! What's your name?" or "Want to play with me?" we are being just like Jesus. We are doing what He tells us to do in John 15:12: "Love each other as I have loved you." Do you want to be like Jesus? Sure, you do. Then don't forget the lesson of Jenny and Rabbie, and don't forget the friends who reached out to me in my wheelchair.

When you make a friend of someone who's not like everyone else, who's a little *different,* you not only help that person, but you become a better "you"—because you're loving the way Jesus loves!

Joni Eareckson Tada

Some of Joni's friends visit her on her radio program.